Nicholas

Catherine Grantham

CONTRIBUTIONS BY ELI ALLEN
ILLUSTRATED BY SUSAN PELTIER

No one thinks that many people will remember them or what they do. But this story will show how an act of kindness will stay in our hearts forever.

During the 4th century, a young priest named Nicholas lived in the town of Myra, Lycia, Asia Minor, now called Turkey. He was a kind and generous young man. The people of the town of Myra knew him from the good things he did. He never looked for thanks or made a big deal out of things he helped with. They called him Father Nicholas.

One cold December night Father Nicholas heard the town Cobbler say he couldn't feed his three daughters and worried about their future. Now, a Cobbler is someone who makes shoes for everyone. Times were hard in the town and he wasn't selling many shoes.

Father Nicholas's heart was sad for the Cobbler and his daughters. He lay awake praying for a way to help the family. So, the next evening, as it got dark, he hurried to the Cobbler's house and secretly dropped a bag of gold coins through the window. The coins landed in some shoes by the fire.

The next morning the family found the gold coins and were so surprised and happy. The Cobbler, who didn't cry easily, found his eyes wet with thankfulness. "Bless the kind soul who gave us this miracle," he said.

News of the happy event spread throughout Myra very quickly. Father Nicholas walking by the Cobbler's later, stopped to hear about the family's happiness, but he kept quiet about what he had done.

As time went on, more stories of unexpected help would be heard in the town, especially when December's cold came. A widow found her pantry full of food, a farmer's debts were paid, and children discovered toys and sweets in their shoes.

This simple act of leaving gifts in shoes grew into a powerful act of community kindness. Nicholas' act of dropping the gold coins into the shoes of the Cobbler turned into a town-wide expression of caring for their neighbor. Soon shoes, of all sizes and shapes, for children and adults, appeared on the doorsteps of homes. The next morning, they would be filled with sweets, toys, coins, or food. Neighbors watched out for each other. They shared food, clothing, and even firewood to keep warm. This generosity and kindness grew into a way of life in the town and over time the story of these secret acts spread to many other places around the world.

Father Nicholas became a guardian angel to his hometown. He inspired goodwill and celebration that shaped the name of Santa Claus as a symbol of joy, hope, and unselfish giving to others. This 'Spirit of Christmas' has continued for more than 17 centuries. Although Father Nicholas is now known as Saint Nicholas, the Wonderworker, he has many other names too. He has been called Father Christmas in England, Sinterklaas in Holland, and Santa Claus in the United States. He is celebrated in December every year.

The shoes were left out for Saint Nicholas to fill with gifts. Later, this became a tradition of hanging stockings by the fireplace instead of placing shoes by the door.

The celebrations added the decorated evergreen trees in Germany during Medieval times. This spirit and tradition came to the United States about four hundred years ago by the Dutch when they immigrated to New Amsterdam now called New York City.

We now celebrate the tradition of giving on Christmas Day, Jesus' birthday, when Love Himself was Born.

The End

Santa Claus Around the World

Afghanistan: Baba Chaghaloo, Papa Noël (بابا نویل)
Africa: Kersvader
Albania: Babai i Krishtlindjeve
Algeria: Sinterklaas
Andorra: Pare Noel
Angola: Santa Claus
Antigua: Santa Claus
Arabia: Mar Nkoula
Argentina: Papá Noel
Armenia: Dzmer Papik (Ձմեռ Պապիկ), Gaghant Baba (Գաղանթ Բաբա)
Australia: Bubaa Gaadha, Santa Claus, Wangkarnal Crow
Austria: Nikolo, Saint Nikolaus
Azerbaijan: Şaxta Baba
Bangladesh: Sāntā klaja (সান্তা ক্লজ)
Basque: San Nikolas
Belarus: Dzied Maroz (Дзед Мароз), Śviaty Mikałaj
Belgium: Père Noël, Sinterklaas, St Nicholas
Bolivia: Papá Noel
Bosnia: Božić Bata, Djed Božićnjak, Djed Mraz
Brazil: Bom Velhinho, Papai Noel
Bulgaria: Dyado Koleda (Дядо Коледа)
Canada: Père Noël, Santa Claus
Catalan: Sant Nicolau
Chile: El Viejito Pascuero

China: Shengdan laoren (聖誕老人)
Colombia: Papá Noel
Costa Rica: San Nicolás, Santa Clós
Croatia: Djed Božićnjak, Saint Lucy, Sveti Nikol
Cyprus: Saint Basil the Great (Άγιος Βασίλειος ο Μέγας)
Czech Republic: Svatý Mikuláš
Denmark: Julemanden
Dominican Republic: Papá Noel, Santa Clós
Ecuador: Papá Noel
Egypt: Baba Noel (بابا نويل), Papa Noël
England: Father Christmas, Santa Claus
Estonia: Jõuluvana
Fiji: Santa Claus
Finland: Joulupukki
France: Le Père Janvier, Le Père Noël, Olentzero, Saint Martin, Saint Nicolas, Tad-kozh
Georgia: Tovlis Babua (თოვლის ბაბუა)
Germany: Belsnickel, Knecht Ruprecht, Krampus, Nikolaus, Weihnachtsmann
Ghana: Papa Bronya
Greece: Saint Basil the Great (Άγιος Βασίλειος ο Μέγας)
Haiti: Père Noël, Tonton Nwèl
Honduras: Santa Claus
Hong Kong: Father Christmas, jyutping (聖誕老人), Saint Nicholas, Santa Claus
Hungary: Krampusz, Mikulas, Télapó
Iceland: Jólasveinar

India: Father Christmas, Papa Christmas (ക്രിസ്മസ് പാപ്പ), Saanta Kloz (सांता क्लॉज़), Saint Nikolas (सैंट निकोलस), Santa Claus

Indonesia: Sant Claus, Sinterklas

Iran: Amu Nowruz (عمو نوروز), Baba Noel (بابا نویل), Bābā Nowruz (بابا نوروز), Santa Claus

Iraq: Baba Noel

Ireland: Daidí na Nollag, Santa Claus, Father Christmas

Italy: Babbo Natale, Saint Lucy

Jamaica: Father Christmas

Japan: Santa Kurōsu (サンタクロース), Santa-san (サンタさん)

Kenya: Baba Krismasi, Santa Claus

Korea: Santa Harabeoji (산타 할아버지), Santa Kullosu (산타 클로스)

Lapland: Korvatunturl

Latvia: Ziemassvētku Vecītis

Lebanon: Baba Noel (بابا نویل), Père Noël

Liberia: Old Man Bayka

Lithuania: Kalėdų Senelis

Luxembourg: Klees'chen

Macedonia: Babagjyshi, Dedo Mraz (Дедо Мраз)

Madagascar: Dadabe Noely, Père Noël

Malta: Father Christmas

Mexico: Santa Claus

Netherlands: Kerstman, Sinterklaas, Zwarte Piet

New Zealand: Hana Kōkō, Santa Claus

Norway: Julenissen, Pa Norsk

Pakistan: Santa Claus (سانتا کلاز)
Panama: Santa Claus
Paraguay: Papá Noel
Persia: Uncle Nowruz عمو نوروز
Perú: Papá Noel, Santa Claus
Philippines: Santa Klaus
Poland: Gwiazdor (Star Man), Santa Claus, Święty Mikołaj
Portugal: Pai Natal, Santa Claus
Romania: Moş Crăciun, Moş Gerilă, Moş Nicolae
Russia: Baboushka, Ded Moroz (Дед Мороз), Grandfather Winter (Кыш Бабай), Grandpa of Yamal (Ямал Ири), Kolyáda, Lord of the Cold (Чысхаан), Saint Nicholas
Scotland: Bodach na Nollaig, Santa Claus
Serbia: Christmas Brother (Božić Bata), Deda Mraz (Деда Мраз)
Slovakia: Svätý Mikuláš
Slovenia: Božiček, Dedek Mraz, Miklavž
South Africa: Father Christmas, Santa Claus, Sinterklaas, uFata Khisimusi
Spain: Apalpador, Olentzero, Papá Noel
Sri Lanka: Naththal Seeya නත්තල් සීයා
Sudan: Cāṇṭā kiḷās (சாண்டா கிளாஸ்)
Sweden: Julbock, Jultomten
Switzerland: Père Noël, Saint Nicholas, Samichlaus
Syria: Baba Noel (بابا نويل)
Taiwan: Old Man of Christmas (聖誕老公公)
Tanzania: Baba Krismasi, Santa Claus
Thailand: Santa Claus (ซานตาคลอส)

Tonga: Sanitā Kolosi
Turkey: Grandfather Gaxan, Noel Baba
Turkmenistan: Aýaz Baba
Ukraine: Did Moroz (Дід Мороз), Sviatyj Mykolaj (Святий Миколай)
United States: Santa Claus, Kris Kringle, Saint Nicholas, Kanakaloka (Hawaiian), Késhmish Hastiin (Navajo)
Uruguay: Papá Noel
Uzbekistan: Ayoz Bobo, Qor Bobo
Venezuela: San Nicolás
Vietnam: Old Man of Christmas (Ông Già Nô-en)
Wales: Chimney John (Siôn Corn), Father Christmas, Santa Claus
Yugoslavia: Dedo Mraz
Zimbabwe: Santa Claus

In gratitude to St. Nicholas, whose spirit of generosity and love for his neighbors has inspired timeless traditions for over 1,700 years.

May his magnificent legacy continue to illuminate the path of kindness in our souls and live on within us all.

Born on March 15, 270
Died on December 6, 343

St. Nicholas was canonized by Pope Eugene IV on June 5, 1446 and became known as the patron saint for children and sailors.

Merry Christmas